CARS ON MARS

and
49
Other
Poems
for
Kids
on
Earth

For Sam —

cars on mars
and
49 other Poems for
Kids on
Earth

by J.D. Landis

Drawings by Denise Landis

[signature]

PUBLISHINGWORKS, INC.
Exeter, NH

2010

PublishingWorks, Inc.,
60 Winter Street
Exeter, NH 03833
603-778-9883

For Orders:
www.revolutionbooksellers.com
1-800-738-6603 or 603-772-7200

Designed by: K. Mack

LCCN: 2007940997

ISBN: 1-933002-62-X
ISBN-13: 978-1-933002-62-0

For Emma and Toby

When you are old enough to read

I hope these poems will succeed

In making you go *Ha Ha Ha*--

I love you both. Signed, Your Grandpa

Contents

The Hello Poem

Hello, I'm a poem
And here's what I do.
I sing and I dance and
I tell you what's true.

What's true about turtles
And earmuffs and gum
And how you or I can
Turn into a plum.

What's true on a planet
So distant in space
We wonder who lives in
That puzzling place.

What's true about brothers
So stupid they're smart
And sisters so close
You can't tell them apart

And bats who play baseball
And whales who can speak
And one girl so lazy
She'd sleep for a week

And while she was sleeping
She'd dream she was...wait!
Check it out for yourself
On page fifty-eight.

Yes, I'm just one poem
Who danced in Jim's drawer.
Now please turn the page to
Find forty-nine more!

A Witch

A witch has landed in
  my room.
She flies around upon her
  broom.
And then she stops and sweeps the floor
And folds my sweatshirts in my drawer
And hangs up my green corduroys
And puts away my thousand toys
And tucks me nicely into bed
And kisses me upon the head
And leaves me feeling snug and calm.
She flies away. I say, "Thanks, Mom!"

Gum

There's gum on my lip.
There's gum in my hair.
There's gum on my shoes.
There's gum on my chair.

There's gum on my eyebrow.
There's gum in my nose.
There's gum on me everywhere
Including my clothes.

There's gum on my sweater.
There's gum on my shirt.
There's gum in my sock.
There's gum under my skirt.

There's gum so many places
There's even a chance
That I've got some gum
On my underpants.

There's gum on my finger.
It's under my nail.
And even my cat's
Got gum on her tail.

There's gum on my desk.
There's gum in my bed.
I'm covered with gum
From my feet to my head.

There's gum on me everywhere,
East, west, north, and south.
But there one place gum's missing--
There's no gum in my mouth.

So excuse me a moment
While I unwrap a stick.
I'm starting to chew it.
Crack, crack! Click, click!

Chompa chomp, chompa chomp.
Slurpedy slurp.
Crackedy, clickedy,
Burpedy burp.

Slippedy, sloppedy,
Chewedy chew.
I've got plenty of gum.
Here's some for you.

What! You don't want it!
You're refusing this gum?
I don't understand that.
Please tell me how come.

I Can't Figure It Out

What am I here for?
What shall I do?
When do I start?
When am I through?
What's a good reason
To get out of bed?
Who is that person
Inside my head?
When will I learn who
I'm going to be?
How will I tell if
That person is me?
Who is the I who's
The I who I know?
Will I ever be
The star of the show?
Why am I sometimes
Scared when I see
Someone who's also
Scared to see me?
How will I know if
I fail or succeed?
Where will I find all
The answers I need?
How can I live with
This infinite doubt?
How will I ever
Figure life out?

Kissing the Animals

I'd like to kiss an elephant,
I'd climb right up its trunk.
I'd like to kiss a platypus.
I'd even kiss a skunk.

I'd love to kiss a tiger,
I'd watch out for its teeth.
I'd even kiss a hippo,
But not from underneath.

I'd kiss a chubby piggy, too,
It couldn't make me fatter.
I'll kiss that endless thin giraffe
By climbing up a ladder.

To kiss a giant polar bear
Would give me quite a chill.
To kiss a wary porcupine
Might give my nose a quill.

I'll kiss a zebra on a stripe,
A leopard on a spot.
I'll kiss a fox while music plays
And we dance the fox-trot.

I'd like to kiss a little lamb,
But not one that's been shorn.
I'll kiss a rhino on its lips
But not, I think, its horn.

I'd love to kiss an antelope
And chase down a gazelle.
I'll kiss a hairy buffalo
If I can stand the smell.

I'll kiss a hamster in its cage,
A lizard in the grass.
I'll travel to a dusty farm
To kiss some big jackass.

I'll kiss a seal, I'll kiss a deer,
I'll kiss a cow, of course.
I'll even dive into the sea
To kiss a sweet sea horse.

I'll kiss a wild wildebeest,
In other words a gnu.
But of all the creatures in the world
I'd most like to kiss you.

The Hat

I came upon a hat one day
As big as all outdoors.
I climbed onto that giant hat.
Why not? A boy explores.

I walked around its giant brim.
I gazed into its chasm.
And then I leaped into its depths
With great enthusiasm.

I found myself alone down there.
It was the finest feeling.
I knew this was the place to live,
A room without a ceiling.

I ran around, I jumped for joy,
I covered every inch.
I knew no one could get me out,
Not even with a winch.

A million people gathered there,
Upon that giant brim.
They called to me, they prayed for me,
They even sang a hymn.

My so-called friends looked down at me
And asked if they could come.
I shook my head and watched them go
Back where they had come from.

Policemen tried to rescue me,
They lowered some long rope.
But nothing could get down that far.
I smiled and said, "Nope."

8

My parents shouted promises.
My teachers shouted lies.
I just looked up at all of them
And said my last goodbyes.

So here I live, within this hat.
It is my home and bed.
And I won't have to leave here till
God puts me on His head.

Watch Out for Those Little Dark Chewy Things

A fly flew right into my ice cream.
I was shocked at behavior so brazen.
And you can be sure I'd have picked it right out
If I hadn't been eating rum raisin.

Plum Thankful

I was eating a plum
When I swallowed the pit.
I thought, "Is this it?
Will I choke on this pit?
Will it shut off my breath?
Is this what it's like
To smother to death?"

Well, I'm happy to say
That I'm fine, for in sum,
That pit went right down,
And now I'm a plum.

Dare You

Melissa says, "Dare you to jump off that wall."
I laugh and I jump and I pray through it all.

Melissa says, "Dare you to climb up that rope."
I laugh and I climb and I nearly lose hope.

Melissa says, "Dare you to stand in that
   lightning."
I laugh and I stand and it really is frightening.

Melissa says, "Dare you to run through that
   fire."
I laugh and I run and I almost expire.

Melissa says, "Dare you to eat that fat worm."
I laugh and I chew and I feel my guts squirm.

Melissa says, "Dare you to give me a kiss."
As if I'd do anything dangerous as this!

Underpants, Underpants

Underpants, underpants,
Where have you gone?
You're not in the hamper,
You're not on the lawn.
You're not in the drier,
You're not on the fence.
I simply can't find you.
It doesn't make sense.

You're not in my closet,
You're not in my drawer.
You're not on the TV,
You're not on the floor.
I'm like a detective
With no evidence.
I simply can't find you.
It doesn't make sense.

You're not in the basement,
You're not on the stool.
You're not in the hallway,
You're not in the pool.
You're not on my bottom!
Please end this suspense.
I simply can't find you.
It doesn't make sense.

You're not in the kitchen,
You're not on the line.
You're not on my sister,
You know that you're mine.
You're not on the stairway,
You're not in my bed.
You're not in the washer,
You're not on my ...oops!

The Shell Hotel

I have a little turtle.
He lives inside his shell.
I've never seen his head or tail.
I wonder if he's well.

I hope he's not afraid of me.
I'm really very gentle.
I whisper, "Do you own that shell
Or is it just a rental?"

Sometimes he sticks his feet outside
Or are those things his hands?
I watch him very closely and
I ask, "What are your plans?"

I leave him worms and flies and bugs
And sometimes uncooked meat.
And then I sit and watch him 'cause
I hope to see him eat.

But he won't eat in front of me.
I guess he's too polite.
Yet in the morning nothing's left.
I guess he eats at night.

"I want to see your face," I say.
"I want to see your tail."
I beg him to come out for me,
But it's to no avail.

"This really isn't fair," I say.
"You're making me a wreck.
I'm even dressing for you now--
Check out my turtleneck."

Of course he doesn't answer me.
He never says a word.
Sometimes I wonder if I should
Have asked to have a bird.

The Late Show

If only I could
Stay up late
I know I wouldn't
Hesitate
To run around and
Bounce a ball
And play my trumpet
In the hall
And dial on the
Telephone
To people I have
Never known
And order up de-
Liveries
Of twenty pizzas,
Triple-cheese,
And feed our dog what
I can't eat
And feed our cat our
Parakeet
And shoot my slingshot
Through the air
Right at our neighbors'
Underwear
And keep the TV
On all night
So I can watch fat
Wrestlers fight
And lock the bathroom
Door so I
Can wash my hair with
Purple dye
And aim a searchlight
In the street

And hide my sister's
Potty seat
And play the latest
Rock and roll
And hip-hop, rap, and
Blues and soul.
And when the clock tolls
Four a.m.
Then I'll transform my
Stratagem
And dress up like an
Alien
And do each of these
Things again.
Oh, gosh, it would be
So much fun.
I wouldn't bother
Anyone.

So how come I can't
Stay up late?
How come my bedtime's
Half past eight?
It's just not fair to
Treat a kid
As if he'd do what
You forbid.
Oh, please, oh let me
Just this once.
I promise then I'll
Sleep for months.

Why I Love Homework

Homework's silly.
Homework's dumb.
Homework makes
My mind go numb.

Homework's pointless.
What's it for?
Homework's just
the biggest bore.

Homework really
Isn't fair.
It just keeps
You in your chair.

Homework's purpose
Isn't clear.
Homework just
Inspires fear.

Homework's used for
Discipline.
Do it once.
Do it *again*.

Homework teaches
Nothing new.
Homework's stuff
We just went through.

Homework's stupid.
What a waste!
All homework
Should be erased.

I hate...uh, oh,
Here comes Heather!
"Let's do our
Homework together."

Homework's different
With a friend.
I hope it
Won't ever end.

The Store

When Annemarie is turning four
Her father takes her to the store.
He says, "Because your birthday's here
Buy anything you want, my dear.
I mean it--anything at all,
Buy something big or something small,
Buy something heavy, something light,
Indulge your fondest appetite.
Buy something practical...or not.

Buy something no one else has got.
But something that fulfills a dream.
Buy something utterly supreme.
And don't consider the expense--
The price tag's of no consequence.
Your birthday comes but once a year.
Buy *anything*—I'm quite sincere."

"Oh, Daddy!" Annemarie cries out
As she stands there and looks about,
Up and down the crowded aisles,
Filled with men with happy smiles.
"Oh, Daddy!" she exclaims once more,
"I know how much you love this store.
And maybe someday there will be
Some things here that are right for me.
And we can both come back again
And celebrate my birthday then."

She holds his hand as she departs
That store called BIG AL'S AUTO PARTS.

The Anger Poem

I'm the angriest boy in the world.
I'm so angry I think I might burst.
Of all the terrible things you have done
This one is really the worst.

I am angrier than I have been
In all of my years on this planet.
How could you have done the thing that you did?
It's impossible that you would plan it.

I am angry enough to freak out.
I am angry enough to explode.
If you ever, ever do that again,
I'll move to another zip code.

I'm so angry I'm losing my mind.
I'm so angry I can't even speak.
And if you won't say that you're sorry
I swear I won't eat for a week.

I'm angry, I'm angry, I'm angry.
I'm the angriest person on earth.
And it's all your fault, you horrible person.
I hate you for all I am worth.

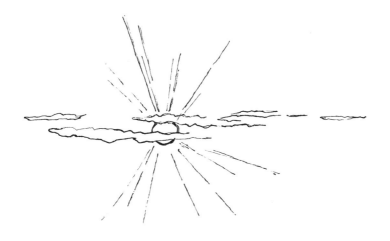

That's so strange, but my anger is gone.
It's as if I just paid a large debt.
If you want my forgiveness, please hurry.
What was it you did? I forget.

Science Lesson

Oh, Harriet, Harriet,
Caught in a lariat,
Roped like a cow
On the range.

Oh, Harriet, Harriet,
Caught in a lariat,
You have to admit
You look strange.

Oh, Harriet, Harriet,
Caught in a lariat,
Swinging around
That big horse.

Oh, Harriet, Harriet,
Caught in a lariat,
Teaching centrif-
Ugal force.

Fat Freddie and the Righteous Rope

In gym they told
Freddie to climb up the rope.
He looked where it went
And then he said, "Nope."

"Climb up it," they said,
"Stop being a brat."
"I can't," said Freddie.
"I'm just too fat."

"Oh, give us a break,"
they hollered at him.
"Climb that rope a few times--
it'll help you get slim."

"I can't," said Freddie.
"I'm afraid that I'll fall."
"Don't worry," they told him.
"We'll catch you, that's all."

So they grabbed hold of Freddie
And lifted his feet.
He could feel their strong arms
Go under his seat.

He was alone on that rope
In a very short time.
They were staring at him
As they all shouted, "Climb!"

The rope hurt his hands
And felt rough on his cheek.
His arms were all shaky,
His legs were all weak.

All that he wanted
Was just to let go.
But he knew if he did that
They'd laugh at him so.

It was too late for laughter,
Too late for disgrace.
Freddie started to climb.
He grew red in the face.

Hand over hand,
Sneaker on sneaker,
He inched his way up
Getting weaker and weaker.

The rope was on fire.
And so was his skin.
He closed both his eyes
So the world wouldn't spin.

"Hey, hurry up, Freddie!"
They called from below.
"You're setting the record--
The record for slow."

Freddie pulled with his arms
And pushed with his feet.
Inside him a drum banged--
Heart beat, heart beat.

The drum helped him climb.
It shut out the sound
Of his terrible enemies
Down on the ground.

And then there it was!
He'd opened his eyes.
The end of the rope.
The ultimate prize.

He reached up to grab it,
That knot in the ceiling.
When his hand closed around it
He felt a strange feeling.

He looked down at himself--
Well, he was still fat...
But light as a feather.
Imagine that!

"All right!" they screamed at him.
"That was one ugly climb.
Now slide your butt down here
And climb up one more time."

"Oh, sure," Freddie yelled back
And let go his grasp.
He could hear the whole gym
Explode with a gasp.

"He's falling!" they screamed.
"He'll die," they predicted.
But Freddie just laughed
As he flew unrestricted.

He floated all over
That smelly old gym.
And then, just as people
Began praising him--
He was, after all, despite his fat face,
The first human being to conquer space--
He floated so comfortably
Right out the door
And never set foot
On this earth any more.

Your Poem

This is your poem.
I write it for you.
Nobody loves you
The way that I do.

Nobody treasures
The bump on your nose.
No one else thinks you've
Got exquisite toes.

No one delights in
Your beautiful mole.
I think without it
You wouldn't be whole.

Nobody tells you
they love how you dress.
I think your clothes are
A smashing success.

No one else cares for
Your gigantic shoes.
Put them on my lap
Whenever you choose.

No one adores how
You always walk fast.
To me the air's sweet
When you've just rushed past.

No one else praises
That haircut you've got.
They say your hairdresser
Deserves to be shot.

No one really likes
The way that you swear.
I know that sometimes
To curse is to care.

No one else laughs at
Your marvelous jokes.
You and I laugh at
Those humorless folks.

Nobody hears the
Profound things you say.
I want to listen
All night and all day.

No one else worships
The person you are.
If I were the sky
You'd be my one star.

This is your poem.
I wrote it for you.
No one could love you
As much as I do.

The Happy Clock

Some nights when I can't fall asleep
And I don't feel like counting sheep
I leave my bed and take a walk
Until I reach the Happy Clock.

The Happy Clock does not keep time.
The Happy Clock won't ever chime.
The Happy Clock will never say
If it is night or it is day.

The Happy Clock does not have hands
Or slowly falling silent sands
Or numbers that your eyes can see
To register time's tyranny.

The Happy Clock is unconcerned
With how some things can't be returned,
Like happy moments you have spent
Or how your future came and went.

The Happy Clock does not exist
To tell you what you might have missed
Or where you might not ever go
Because you always go too slow.

The Happy Clock's the only place
Where you and time aren't in a race
To see just who can finish last
And keep the future from the past.

The Happy Clock is where you see
The meaning of eternity.
The Happy Clock is where you learn
That going forth is to return.

The Happy Clock is where you find
The you whom you have left behind.
And in this great discovery
You realize you have ceased to be.

Oh, Happy Clock, I love you so.
I wish I never had to go
Back to this world where I know I'm
Running quickly slowly out of into time.

Nails for Sales

I used to bite my fingernails,
But now I never do.
I bit them every chance I got.
That's why they never grew.

My parents said they had a cure--
A cure that never fails--
They promised me a hundred bucks...
Check out my nine-inch nails!

The Baseball Bat

Said Jack, "Let's have a baseball game.
Let's meet down at the park."
Said Mary Lou, "I've got a glove."
"I've got a ball," said Mark.

"I've got some baseball shoes with spikes,"
Said Debbie to the rest.
"And I know lots of cheerleaders,"
Said Hank, who was a pest.

"I've got some uniforms," said Jill,
"And they include a hat."
"That's great," said Rick. "This means that all
We're missing is a bat."

"So who will bring a bat?" asked Pam.
"Is there a volunteer?"
The new kid slowly raised his hand.
His name was Vladimir.

So Vladimir rushed home and asked
His parents for a bat.
They clapped their hands. They jumped for joy.
They said, "Imagine that!"

And Vladimir was very pleased
To see his parents glad.
They handed him a bag and said,
"The bat's inside there, Vlad."

He took the bag down to the park.
The other kids were there.
He opened up the bag and the
Bat flew into the air.

It chased the kids from base to base.
It nailed them at the plate.
And Vlad was very proud that his
Bat played the game so great.

"Baseball's really fun," he said.
"It's really where it's at."
That night he thanked his parents for
His wicked baseball bat.

The Wind

Jessica wanted
To ride on the wind.
She got on its back
And quickly unpinned
Her feet from the earth,
Her hair from the air.
She said to the wind,
"I'll go anywhere."

"Anywhere? Sure," said
The wind in her ear.
"Hang on really tight or
You'll fall off, my dear."
So Jessica held on
With all of her might
As the wind awooshed
Them into the night.

They flew over land,
They flew over sea,
And Jessica screamed,
"How great to be free!"
They flew right through clouds
That gurgled with rain.
They flew among birds
Who raced them in vain.

They flew to the moon
And then on to Mars.
They flew far away,
Beyond all the stars.
They flew to the edge
Of the universe.
And that's when the wind
Went into reverse.

"Keep going!" she said.
"Don't stop now, you fool!
The next thing I know
I'll land back in school!"
"Oh, my," said the wind,
"That simply won't do.
Might there be some place
Where I can drop you?"

"Not really," she said.
"I'm not letting go.
I just want a ride
Wherever you blow."

And so she remains
Aloft in the sky.
No one can find her,
Not you and not I.

The Lowly Mosquito

The lowly mosquito
Is awfully maligned.
She buzzes and dive bombs
And bites your behind
Or flies round your ear
And flies round it again.
She even drives nuts
People practicing Zen.
You often don't feel her
Until she has dipped
Her mean little nose
Into where you're unzipped.
And then you scream, "Ouch!"
And you slap where you're bited--
That mosquito has fled
Like a guest uninvited.
But if you should hit her
You still feel quite cruddy
When you lift up your palm
And discover it's bloody.
Revenge is a game
Played in all kinds of wars,
But with a mosquito
The blood's always yours.
And even long after
That creature is dead,
She leaves her own tombstone
You scratch till it's red.
She really proves Nature
Is awfully malicious.
How else to explain
Why she finds us delicious?
When Man's time has come
And he's truly finito,
His blood will live on--
In the lowly mosquito.

Earmuffs

I always wear my earmuffs.
I wear them day and night.
I wear them everywhere I go.
I wear them extra tight.

My girlfriend doesn't like me
To wear them when I date her.
"Why," she asks, "wear earmuffs when
We live near the Equator?"

My earmuffs aren't for comfort.
That's not what they're about.
I wear them 'cause without them
I've got ears that stick waaaaaaaaaaaaay out.

The Dimple

She had a dimple in her chin.
It went an awfully long way in.
She liked to put her finger there.
It disappeared with room to spare.

She wondered how deep it might be
And found a way that she could see.
One day she pulled it inside out.
Now if she turns her head...watch out!

Too Long a Shower

One day I took a shower
And stayed in there so long
That when I was all finished
I knew something was wrong.

I couldn't see my body.
I thought it was a dream.
Where once I had been standing
Now there was only steam.

I looked into the mirror.
I was no longer there.
I'd turned into a fog bank.
I'd even lost my hair!

I had evaporated.
I'd gone right up in smoke.
I'd been warned this could happen.
I'd thought it was a joke.

My parents always told me
To keep my showers brief.
But no, I'd never listened,
And now I'd come to grief.

I walked out of the bathroom
And drifted down the stairs.
My parents and their guests sat
Completely unawares.

I floated in among them.
Their voices were not loud,
Until my father shouted,
"Look there! I see a cloud!"

My mother said, "Oh, Eddie,
You really mustn't dream."
And then she turned and saw me.
She loosed a mighty scream.

The others at the table
Could not believe their eyes.
They pointed and they whispered.
That's when I yelled, "Surprise!"

They all jumped in their seats then.
They turned as white as chalk.
I finally heard a man say,
"Good grief, that cloud can talk!"

Another man said, "Nonsense.
That isn't what we hear.
No cloud has ever spoken.
We've all had too much beer."

"Oh, no," I said. "That's not true.
It's me, and I can speak."
My mother said, "It's Jimmy!"
Her best friend shouted, "Eeek!"

"What's happened to you, Jimmy?"
My parents asked at once.
And they went on together,
"Is this one of your stunts?"

"Oh, no," I said, "it isn't.
I truly have transgressed.
I took too long a shower,"
I ruefully confessed.

"He took too long a shower!"
The other people groaned.
"You mean you never told him
Long showers aren't condoned?"

"Of course we did!" my parents
Informed their gathered friends.
"But Jimmy didn't listen.
Now look at how it ends.

"Our son's become a vapor.
Our son's become a mist.
Oh, whatever shall we do?
He shortly won't exist."

I really missed my parents.
Though I remained right there.
I knew that soon I'd vanish,
Invisible as air.

And so I started crying.
I croaked just like a frog.
But even salty teardrops
Can never melt a fog.

Just then a door flew open.
It must have been the wind.
It said, "Too long a shower?
Oh, son, you've truly sinned."

That wind blew like a demon
With an ungodly howl.
And when it died down, someone
Screamed, "Hurry, get a towel!"

I stood there in my glory,
Not meaning to be rude.
The wind had finally freed me.
Except I was...well, nude.

I said, "I've learned my lesson.
I've felt the wind's great wrath.
Now if you'll all excuse me...
I think I'll take a bath."

44

My Little Kitty

I had a little kitty.
She had a litter box.
It really was a pity.
She much preferred my socks.

I Once Had a Parrot

I once had a parrot
Who ate only carrot.
I thought that was terribly funny.

Till he leapt from his cage
And as if on a stage
Went hopping around like a bunny.

Cars on Mars

When I look at the sky at night
I wonder what's out there.
I wonder if there's people
And if their heads have hair.

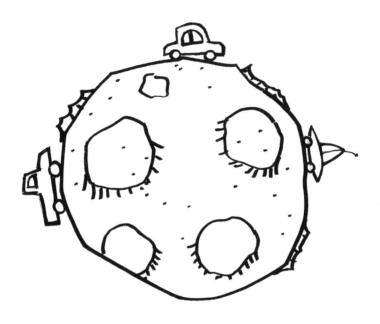

I wonder if they dress like us
Or wear their birthday suits
And if they walk around in space
Or fly with parachutes.

I wonder if they love their kids
And give them lots of toys
And if they know the difference
Between the girls and boys.

I wonder if their animals
Are like the ones down here
Or if their Santa uses pigs
Instead of eight reindeer.

I wonder who their friends are
And if they ever fight
And if they want to punish someone
Just because she's right.

I wonder what goes on up there
Way off among the stars,
If they have dogs on Pluto,
If they have cars on Mars.

The Mirror

One morning I looked in the mirror
And somebody looked back at me
Who wasn't the usual fellow
That I was accustomed to see.

An old man stood staring right at me.
He wore an old suit and a tie.
The hat on his head looked quite silly.
And there was a tear in his eye.

He seemed just as startled as I was
And just as unable to speak.
We stood there amazed at each other
As if we were watching a freak.

"Who are you?" I found myself saying,
"And what are you doing in there?
How did you end up in my mirror?
It's hardly a thing we can share."

His lips moved as if he were speaking.
But I couldn't hear any sound.
He motioned for me to move closer.
I did. My heart started to pound.

He softly said, "This is my mirror.
I didn't expect to find you.
Each morning I look at myself here.
I'm old--that's a hard thing to do."

I couldn't believe what he told me.
I said, "But this mirror is mine!
Each morning I look at myself here.
I'm young, so I want to look fine."

"You *do*!" he said with great excitement.
"You look so much better than I.
I wish you could stay young forever.
I wish..." Then he started to cry.

"I'm sorry you're trapped in that mirror,"
I said. "I don't know what to do."
He looked at me sadly and answered,
"If anyone's trapped here, it's you.

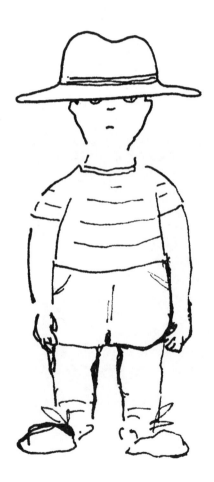

"I see you don't realize who I am.
I recognized you instantly.
I am the same person as you are.
And you, my young fellow, are me.

"A mirror is merely a window
Through which every child must climb.
Your enemy waits right inside it.
And that enemy is called Time."

As if to prove he wasn't lying,
He took off his hat from his head.
"You see, we look just like each other."
And that was the last thing he said.

"Please wait!" I cried into the mirror.
Too late. He had faded from view.
"Come back!" I called into the mirror.
"There's so much I want to ask you."

Sometimes I think this never happened.
Sometimes I prefer it like that.
But what do I say to my parents
When they ask me where I got this hat?

The Fashion Critic

My sister put on make-up
And then a party dress.
She asked, "How do I look now?"
I answered, "You're a mess."

She wiped off all her make-up
And changed into some pants.
She asked, "Do I look better?"
I answered, "Not a chance."

She brushed her hair in ringlets,
Pulled on a pair of tights.
She asked, "Do you prefer this?"
I screamed, "Turn off the lights!"

She wrapped her neck in diamonds,
Put on a formal gown.
She asked, "Do I look pretty?"
I gave her two thumbs-down.

So she put on her bathrobe
And stayed at home with me.
I said, "Why, you're so
    thoughtful
    To keep me company."

My Stupid Brother

I call my brother stupid.
He really is a jerk.
I'm goofing with my buddies,
He's doing his homework.

I'm skipping all my classes
And going to the pool.
That sucker never misses
A single day of school.

I'm chasing after hubcaps
And playing chute-the-chute.
He's learning mathematics
And practicing the flute.

I'm dreaming of the time when
I'll stay in bed all day.
My brother's busy building
A model of Pompeii.

I love to spend the weekend
All loose down at the mall.
That wimp is at the museum
Copying Chagall.

I'm eating lots of pizza
And drinking lots of Cokes.
My brother's separating
The egg whites from the yolks.

I can't wait till I'm older
So I can go to bars.
My brother's dumb ambition's
To travel to the stars.

He's really such a loser.
I feel bad for that dude.
He wishes he could do like me
And get himself tattooed.

I'm hanging with my buddies
And throwing rocks at squirrels.
My brother--what a doofus!--
Gets chased around by girls.

He's probably adopted.
How else can you explain
Why I am such a genius
And he ain't got no brain?

I'd really like to help him.
There's so much I could do,
If only once he'd say to me,
"I'd like to be like you."

Left or Right?

Galloping Pete
Was born with three feet.
He loved having more than his share.

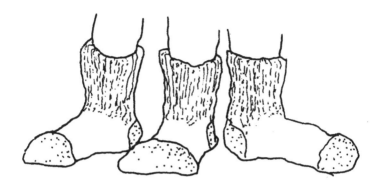

But when shopping for shoes,
His Mom got the blues,
When she tried to buy 1 1/2 pair.

Up a Tree

I climbed up in a tree one day
And then decided I would stay.
I liked the view from way up there.
When it got dark I didn't care.
When I got hungry I could eat
Some berries that grew near my feet.
The leaves played music in my ears.
I thought, "I think I'll stay for years."
Not that there's much else you
  can do
When on the ground things
  wait for you.

Y Im Purfkt

Thay teech us howda spel in skul.
I alwaz wundur y.
Therz not a wurd thet I kant spel.
I nevur hafta tri.

Its tru I kan spel ani wurd.
I nevur mak miztaks.
I ges thets y mi techur sez
I giv thu clas hedaks.

Lazy Lizzie

They call me Lazy Lizzie,
I can't imagine why.
I get up every morning...
Or, at least, I try.

I sometimes put my clothes on,
Depending on my mood.
But if I am too tired...
I dress in the nude.

I walk to school each morning,
Unless I get a ride
Or find I must be absent
'Cause my TV died.

I never do my homework.
It's not that I'm a fool.
But I'm not gonna carry
Homework home from school.

They say I am a sluggard.
I find that quite unjust.
I baked them a nice pie once...
All except the crust.

They say I am lethargic.
I don't know what that means.
Checking dictionaries ain't
Really in my genes.

They call me Lazy Lizzie.
It really isn't right.
I dream I'm moving mountains
Each and every night.

Recipe

You take a dozen chocolate bars
And melt them in a pot.
Then add ten scoops of ice cream
(That's really not a lot).

Throw in a hundred marshmallows--
The number never varies--
But have as many as you like
Of maraschino cherries.

Some butterscotch (you pour it in),
And don't forget the nuts.
Remember first to chop them up--
You mustn't take shortcuts.

Then heat ten sticks of chewing gum
And spread them through the mix.
They'll hold all this together
(You're learning all my tricks).

Now top it off with whipped cream--
A gallon should be plenty--
And sprinkle it with jimmies,
By handfuls measure twenty.

That's it! You've made my favorite dish.
I hope it was great fun.
There's just one more instruction:
This recipe Serves One!

Over My Head

The first time that I saw the sea
I knew it was the place for me.

It was a great big swimming pool
In which I could get nicely cool.

I jumped right in to swim a lap.
I didn't think I'd need a map.

And yet the more I found I'd swum
No nearer to the end I'd come.

I swam and swam and swam and swam
And thought, "I wonder where I am,"

Until I finally met a whale
Who said, "What happened to your sail?"

I answered, "I don't mean to gloat,
But I'm a person, not a boat.

"Now if you'd be so kind, my friend,
And tell me, where does this pool end?"

"Pool!" he screamed. "That's quite a notion.
Don't you know you're in the ocean?"

"Call it what you like," I said,
"As long as I'm not over my head."

The whale said, "Please don't lose much sleep
When I say it's a mile deep."

"A mile deep!" I couldn't look down.
Over my head! I thought I'd drown.

"Rescue me!" I begged of him.
"When I'm over my head, I can't swim."

"Oh, really?" said the whale politely.
"Hop on, kid, and hold on tightly."

I got a ride--I felt so cool--
All the way to the end of that pool.

But it didn't look familiar
And the air was slightly chillier.

"Where am I?" I asked of that whale.

But he just waved his giant tail

And swam away into the sea
Without another word to me.

I missed my parents and my home
Across that watery, windy foam.

And so I went out on a limb
And jumped back in and took a swim.

I swam across that ocean wide.
It was a very tiring ride.

But finally I got back to shore
And went home and knocked on the door.

Mother screamed, "I thought you were dead!"
Father screamed, "You went over your head!"

"Yes, everything you say is true,"
I said. "But I've come home to you."

They hugged me and put me to bed.
I'd learned to swim--over my head.

The Newest Member of the Football Team

No sooner do I go to bed
When something lands upon my head.

I close my eyes and fall asleep.
Whatever's on my head will keep.

But then I have the strangest dream:
They put me on the football team.

And when I wake up the next day,
The kids all ask me out to play.

The Food Chain

Worms are luscious.
What a treat.
Worms are so much
Fun to eat.

Watch them wiggle.
Watch them squirm.
Nothing tempts me
Like a worm.
I like brown ones.
I like gray.
I'll eat pink ones
Any day.

Long ones, short ones,
Thin ones, fat,
Some are round and
Some are flat.

Some are juicy,
Some are dry.
Worms, they always
Satisfy.

"Ugh!" you say? Well,
Pardon me.
You eat worms when
You eat me.

Friendship Is the Greatest Bargain

My best friend's name is Shanika.
She never screams or hollers.
Can you believe she'd be that nice
And only cost four dollars?

So What Else Is New?

I had a little pimple.
It didn't make me frantic.

So tell me--why'd I squeeze it?
For now it's grown gigantic!

The Perfect Kid

I've never made a mistake.
I've never done anything wrong.
I've never messed up the tiniest thing.
I've always been right all along.

I've never gotten a grade
That wasn't the best in my school.
I've never broken a promise.
I've never broken a rule.

I've never once misbehaved.
I've never been punished at all.
I've never been told that I blundered or erred.
I've never once fumbled the ball.

I've never been out of line.
I've never committed faux pas.
And I've not one time in my eight years on earth
Been involved in a big brouhaha.

I've never had to be told
Anything like a direction.
There's only one word for a person like me
And that one word is this: perfection.

I've never had any friends.
I've never met someone like me.
I wish I could find just one other kid
Who does everything perfectly.

My First Watch

My parents bought me my first watch.
They said, "This will tell time."
I listen to it day and night--
It doesn't even chime.

"Please talk to me," I say to it.
"Please tell me what you know."
But my new watch won't even say
If it runs fast or slow.

I look at it and get confused.
Its numbers go around.
Its little sticks keep moving but
They never make a sound.

It's never told me anything.
I've listened for three weeks.
How can a watch tell time if it's
So rude it never speaks?

Bad Medicine

There was a young man from Brazil
Who swallowed the wrong kind of pill.
It made him turn blue.
It could happen to you.
And if you take the wrong pill it will.

Starvation Diet

There was once a fat man from Madrid
Who was told to eat nothing but squid.
He chewed and he chewed.
He chewed and he chewed.
But of squid he could never get rid.

Abraham's Song

I would just as soon
Be a balloon
And fly away
Every day.

I would just as well
Be a clam shell
And close up tight
Every night.

I would with pleasure
Be a treasure
And fall asleep
Mine to keep.

I would quite nicely
Be precisely
The boy I am
Abraham.

Fast Food

The fastest food I ever saw
Ran so fast it broke the law.
Hamburgs, onions, pickles, fries,
I could not believe my eyes.
Every golden chicken nugget
Ran so fast I couldn't hug it.
Every single fish fillet
Winked at me and ran away.
Even things like Happy Meals
Zoomed right by as if on wheels.
Not to mention shakes and sodas--
They went faster than Toyotas.
All the food you'd ever want
Ran out of the restaurant.

I chased that food until I tripped.
I scraped my hand. My pants were ripped.
And that's how I found out it's true:
Fast food isn't good for you!

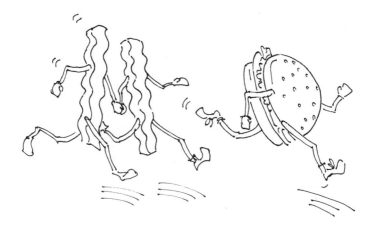

I've Run Out of Rhymes

I've run out of rhymes,
I've run out of rhymes.
Of all the bad times,
I've run out of rhymes.

I'm sitting alone
Right here in my home.
I live in a dome.
My hair needs a comb.
I'm writing a

A what? A what? A what? A what?
Oh, why must a poet just sit on his

I've run out of rhymes,
I've run out of rhymes.
Of all the bad times,
I've run out of rhymes.

There's so much to say.
I write every day.
I'd much rather play.
This work doesn't pay,
Especially when
The rhymes go away.

Of all
Of all
The terrible crimes,
To say you're a poet
And run out of

Of what? Of what? Of what? Of what?
I think every poet must be a real

Writing verse
Is so perverse.
Call the doctor,
Call the
The what? The what? The what? The what?
Oh why must a poet just sit on his

What did you say? What did you say?
You be the poet. I'm going

I Think I Finally Figured It Out

Life is a question.

You are the answer.

J. D. Landis is a silly (but in a good way) man who loves children (his own, but not alone), poetry, his wife (what an artist!), animals, vegetables (except beets), minerals, and everything else (almost) on Earth (and on Mars).

He is the author of the novels *Lying in Bed*, which won the Morton Dauwen Zabel Award from the American Academy of Arts and Letters, *Longing*, which was a New York Times Notable Book, and *Artist of the Beautiful*. His work has been published as well in England, Germany, Italy, The Netherlands, and Portugal.

He has also published six novels for young readers, including *The Sisters Impossible*, which was an International Reading Association Children's Choice. For many years he worked in book publishing and was Publisher and Editor-in-Chief of William Morrow & Company in New York.

This particular silly man lives in Exeter, New Hampshire.

When she isn't drawing, Denise Landis spends her time cooking and gardening. She is the author of the *New York Times* cookbook *Dinner for Eight: 40 Great Dinner Party Menus for Friends and Family*. She has four children and is married to a silly man who shows her his poetry before he shows it to anyone else.